DINOFOURS®
Color-Word Storybook

IT'S REST TIME!

by Steve Metzger
Illustrated by Hans Wilhelm

SCHOLASTIC INC.
New York   Toronto   London   Auckland   Sydney
Mexico City   New Delhi   Hong Kong   Buenos Aires

To Phil Bender
—S.M.

Go to www.scholastic.com for Web site information on Scholastic authors and illustrators.

ISBN 0-439-32047-X

12 11 10 9 8 7 6 5 4 3 2 1   01 02 03 04 05
Printed in the U.S.A.
First Scholastic printing, October 2001

Help Your Child Learn to Read with Dinofours® Color-Word Storybooks

On this page, you'll find a list of several words in color. Point to the first color word (the word "**blocks**") as you read it to your child. Let your child know that the word "**blocks**" will be red every time it appears in this book. Then have your child repeat the word "**blocks**" back to you. As you read the story, point out each color word to your child.

The first time you read the story, you might want to read it through without using the color-word feature. The second time, you might want to ask your child to read just one of the color words. As your child gains confidence, he or she might want to read a second color word...then a third...then a fourth. It's all up to you and your child!

The color words for this book are:

blocks   **book/books**   **puzzle/puzzles**
rest   **cot/cots**

All morning long, the Dinofours had been very busy in their classroom:

Painting at the easel!

Playing with clay!

Building with **blocks**!

And now... it was **Rest** Time.

"Okay, children," said Mrs. Dee. "You can each take one **book** from the bookshelf and then find a **cot** to **rest** on. I'll lower the lights a bit and put on some music."

Brendan walked over to Mrs. Dee as she put a cassette tape in the tape player.

"But I don't want to **rest**, Mrs. Dee," said Brendan. "I'm not tired."

"I know, Brendan," said Mrs. Dee. "But you've had a very active morning, and now it's time to relax for a while."

Brendan stomped over to a **cot** and sat down. Then he sang this song to himself:

Resting, resting,
On my **cot**.
Do I like it?
I do NOT!

Brendan looked at the other children on their **cots**.
"Good night, everyone!" he called out in his loudest voice. "Pleasant dreams!"
"Be quiet!" said Tara.
"Shhh," said Joshua. "I'm trying to read my **book**."
For a moment, Brendan was quiet.

Then he stood on his **cot** and yelled, "Mrs. Dee! Mrs. Dee!"
Mrs. Dee walked quickly over to Brendan's **cot**.
"What's the matter, Brendan?" she asked.
"I'm bored," Brendan replied.
"Well," said Mrs. Dee. "Would you like to look at a **book**?"
Brendan nodded.
"Good," said Mrs. Dee.

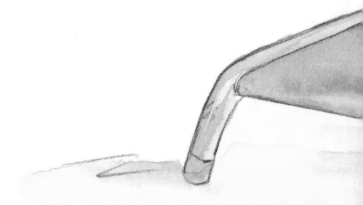

Brendan skipped over to the bookshelf. He couldn't decide
which **book** to take back to his **cot**, so...he took a whole
bunch. Brendan was carrying such a large stack that he couldn't
see where he was going. Just before he reached his **cot**, Brendan
lost his balance. The **books** fell to the floor with a crash!

"Quiet, Brendan!" said Albert.

"Shhh," said Danielle.

Mrs. Dee quickly came over to see what was going on.

"Brendan!" she said. "I said you could take *one* **book**, not so many!"

"But all the **books** looked good," Brendan said. "I didn't know which one to pick."

"Here's a nice one," Mrs. Dee said as she gave Brendan a **book** about a duck that wouldn't fly south for the winter.

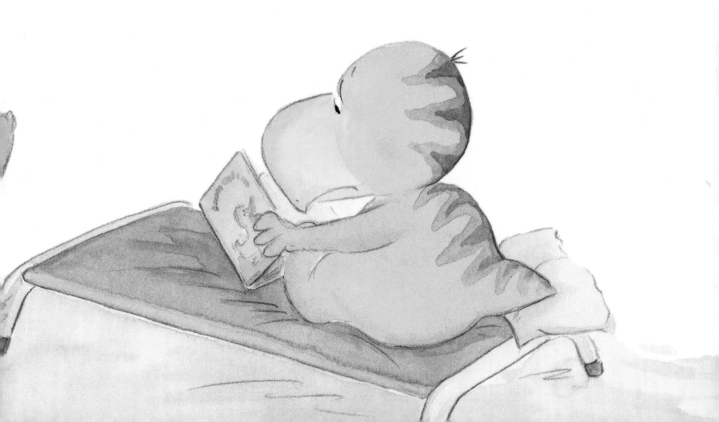

Mrs. Dee returned Brendan's other **books** to the bookshelf. But when she turned around, Brendan and his **cot** weren't there! Mrs. Dee looked around the classroom until she finally found him … right next to Albert and his **cot**. Brendan and Albert were putting together a jigsaw **puzzle**.

"Brendan!" Mrs. Dee said when she arrived next to Brendan's **cot**. "What are you doing over here?"

"I was lonely," Brendan said. "I wanted to play with Albert."

"Brendan was helping me with my **puzzle**," Albert said.

"You'll have plenty of chances to play with your friend later," Mrs. Dee said to Brendan. "But now," she said as she moved his cot back to where it belonged, "you need to stay here."

"All right," Brendan said.

"Brendan," Mrs. Dee said. "I'm going to get our next art project ready. While I'm away, I expect you to rest quietly on your cot."

"I'll try," Brendan said.

Brendan lay down and listened to the music that was coming from the tape player.

"That's nice music," he said. He stood up on his **cot** and started dancing. "I love to dance."

The other children saw Brendan dancing and began to laugh.

"Look at Brendan," said Danielle.

"He's so silly," said Tracy.

Mrs. Dee hurried over and looked at Brendan.

"Brendan, you must stop dancing!" Mrs. Dee said in a firm voice. "This is Rest Time, not dancing time! Do you understand?"

Brendan stopped dancing and lay down on his cot. "Yes, I understand," he said softly.

"Now, I don't expect you to sleep," Mrs. Dee said. "But I *do* expect you to be still on your cot for a while. There are only a few minutes of Rest Time left. And then we'll be making paper bag puppets!"

"I love making puppets!" Brendan said excitedly. "I'm going to make a giant puppet with lots of hair and a big nose. I can't wait."

"That's great," said Mrs. Dee with a smile. "I'll let you know when we're ready."

"Okay," said Brendan. He closed his eyes and imagined how he would make his puppet the biggest one.

Mrs. Dee returned to the art table and put out the materials for the children to make their puppets. There were paper bags, glue, felt scraps, and cotton balls. Then she announced, "All right, children. You can get up now. **Rest** Time is over."

The children got off their **cots**, put their **books** and **puzzles** away, and joined Mrs. Dee at the art table. As they gathered together, Albert looked around the table.

"Mrs. Dee, Mrs. Dee, where's Brendan?" Albert asked.

"Maybe he's in the bathroom," suggested Joshua.

"No," said Tracy. "Brendan's not in the bathroom."

"Maybe he's playing with **blocks**," said Tara.

"No," said Joshua. "Brendan's not in the **blocks** area."

"Maybe he's playing with a **puzzle**," said Danielle.

But Brendan wasn't playing with a **puzzle** either.

"Hmmm," said Mrs. Dee. "I think I know where Brendan is, and it's the last place I expected him to be!"

"Where?" the children all asked.

"Shhh," Mrs. Dee replied. "He's right over there, sound asleep on his **cot**."

The children gathered around Brendan's **cot** to watch him sleep.

"Let's be as quiet as we can and let Brendan sleep a bit longer," Mrs. Dee said. "After all, he's had a *very busy* **Rest** Time!"

Then Brendan began to dream about dancing in the clouds.
In his dream, Brendan sang this song to himself:

> *When I'm dancing way up high,*
> *I hop and skip and leap.*
> *But now I feel so tired that*
> *I'd like to go to sleep!*

Still asleep, Brendan smiled.
"Sleep tight," Mrs. Dee said in a soft voice. "Sweet dreams!"